PRESENTED TO

_____

FROM

_____

_____

HOW TO GET A
DADDY
TO SLEEP

AMY PARKER
ILLUSTRATED BY
NATALIA MOORE

Tommy
NELSON

An Imprint of Thomas Nelson

How to Get a Daddy to Sleep

Tommy Nelson, PO Box 141000, Nashville, TN 37214

Published in Nashville, Tennessee, by Tommy Nelson. Tommy Nelson is an imprint of Thomas Nelson. Thomas Nelson is a registered trademark of HarperCollins Christian Publishing, Inc.

Illustrated by Natalia Moore

Tommy Nelson titles may be purchased in bulk for educational, business, fund-raising, or sales promotional use. For information, please e-mail SpecialMarkets@ThomasNelson.com.

Library of Congress Cataloging-in-Publication Data

Names: Parker, Amy, 1976- author. | Moore, Natalia, 1986- illustrator.
Title: How to get a daddy to sleep / Amy Parker ; illustrated by Natalia Moore.
Description: Nashville, Tennessee : Tommy Nelson, [2020] | Audience: Ages 4-8. | Summary: A young child demonstrates how to ensure Daddy will get a good night's rest, such as making him a fancy meal and loudly singing him a lullaby. Includes a prayer.
Identifiers: LCCN 2020004663 | ISBN 9781400214624 (hardcover) | ISBN 9781400214648 (board)
Subjects: CYAC: Stories in rhyme. | Father and child--Fiction. | Bedtime--Fiction. | Christian life--Fiction.
Classification: LCC PZ8.3.P1645 Ho 2020 | DDC [E]--dc23
LC record available at https://lccn.loc.gov/2020004663

Printed in China

20 21 22 23 24   DSC   10 9 8 7 6 5 4 3 2 1

Mfr: DSC / Dongguan, China / August 2020 / PO #9589856

To Daniel, Daddy, Gary, Mr. Parker, Pepa Thomas, Pepa McLain,

Granddaddy, Granddaddy Jim, Granddaddy Young, and

all the daddies who have shown me unlimited wisdom,

unconditional love, and inexhaustible giving, reflecting

the many facets of the most perfect Father of all.

Daddy is a **gift** from God;

He *never* takes a break!

Let's show him how to get some rest—

No matter what it takes!

Make the most of Daddy's time
When he's at home with you;
Be sure to get an **early** start—

You have **so much** to do!

Daddies always need some help
With picking out their clothes;
He'll need some **jewelry** and a **hat**—

He'll look so good

in those!

To help your dad feel special,

Make him a **fancy** meal;

And just this once, he's sure to smile

When he looks at the **bill**!

Be sure Daddy goes outside

To *RUN* and JUMP and wheeee!

Show him the beauty God has made,

Each flower, every tree.

Helping Daddy with his chores

Shows him how much you **care**;

And when the veggies all get ripe,

Maybe you'll even share!

When Daddy washes the car,

Be sure to **lend a hand**!

When you mess up or miss a spot,

He

always

understands!

For an **EXTRA** fun-filled day,

Take Dad to see a game!

Without you cheering **by his side**,

It wouldn't be the same.

And yet even **the best days**

Are rough on Daddy's feet;

Let him sit back, relax, and rest

For his own special **treat**!

When it's finally story time,
He's in for a **surprise**!
Act out a story, just for him—
He won't believe his eyes!

Daddy just can't go to sleep

Without a **lullaby**;

So sing out loud, with **all your heart**;

He'll love how hard you try!

When it's time to say your prayers,

Thank God for **all** your gifts—

And make sure that your daddy is

The **first one**

on the list!

Daddy will fall fast asleep

Because of all you've done;

Tuck him in and **kiss good night**,

Remembering

all the

fun.

Then as he lies there snoring,

Say a quiet thank-you

To Daddy, who adores you so,

No matter what you do.

A Bedtime Prayer for My Daddy & Me

Dear God,
Thank You for my daddy,
The best to ever be!
Protect him, lead him, guide him well,
Just as he does for me.

And, God, please help my daddy
To really find some rest
And spend some time alone with You
So he can be his best!
Amen.

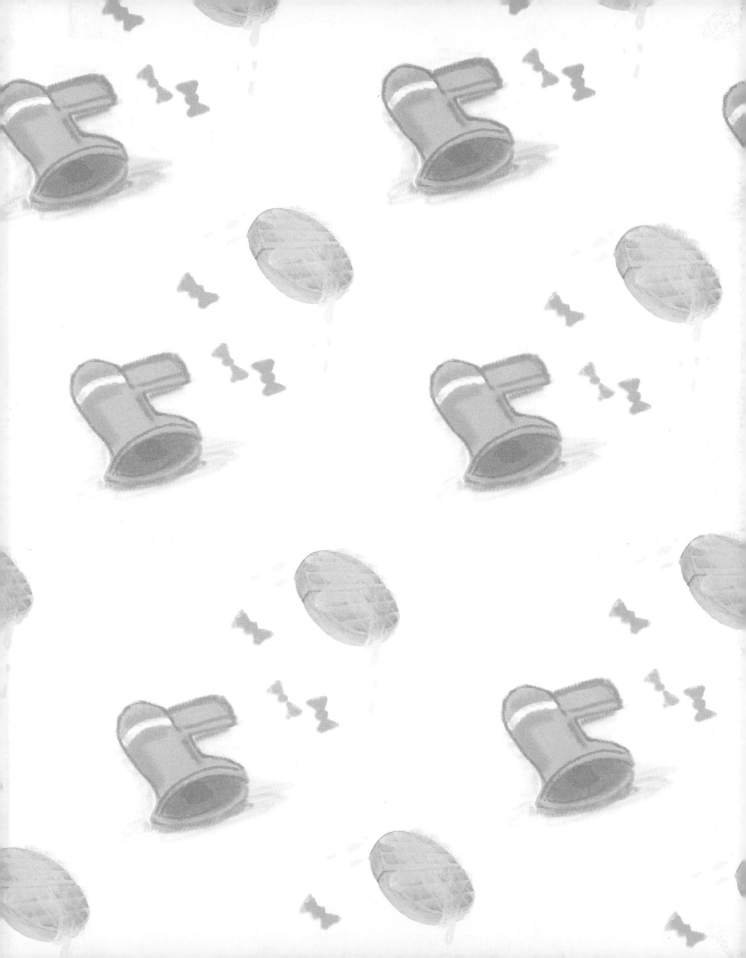